THE STORY OF
A NODDING DONKEY

LAURA LEE HOPE

THE STORY OF A NODDING DONKEY

CHAPTER I

THE SANTA CLAUS SHOP

The Nodding Donkey dated his birth from the day he received the beautiful coat of varnish in the workshop of Santa Claus at the North Pole. Before that he was just some pieces of wood, glued together. His head was not glued on, however, but was fastened in such a manner that with the least motion the Donkey could nod it up and down, and also sidewise.

It is not every wooden donkey who is able to nod his head in as many ways as could the Donkey about whom I am going to tell you. This Nodding Donkey was an especially fine toy, and, as has been said, his first birthday was that on which he received such a bright, shiny coat of varnish.

"Here, Santa Claus, look at this, if you please!" called one of the jolly workmen in the shop of St. Nicholas. "Is this toy finished, now?" and he held up the Nodding Donkey.

Santa Claus, who was watching another man put some blue eyes in a golden-haired doll, came over to the bench where sat the man who had made the Nodding Donkey out of some bits of wood, glue, and real hair for his mane and tail.

"Hum! Yes! So you have finished the Nodding Donkey, have you?" asked Santa Claus, as he stroked his long, white beard.

"I'll call him finished if you say he is all right," answered the man, smiling as he put the least tiny dab more of varnish on the Donkey's back. "Shall I set him on the shelf to dry, so you may soon take him down to Earth for some lucky boy or girl?"

"Yes, he is finished. Set him on the shelf with the other toys," answered dear old St. Nicholas, and then, having given a last look at the Donkey, the workman placed him on a shelf, next to a wonderful Plush Bear, of whom I shall tell you more in another book.

"Well, I'm glad he's finished," said Santa Claus' worker, as he took up his tools to start making a Striped Tiger, with a red tongue. "That Nodding Donkey took me quite a while to finish. I hope nothing happens to him until his coat of varnish is hard and dry. My, but he certainly shines!"

And the Nodding Donkey did shine most wonderfully! Not far away, on the same shelf on which he stood, was a doll's bureau with a looking glass on top. In this looking glass the Nodding Donkey caught sight of himself.

"Not so bad!" he thought. "In fact, I'm quite stylish. I'm almost as gay as some of the clowns." And his head bobbed slowly up and down, for it was fastened so that the least jar or jiggle would move it.

"I must be very careful," said the Nodding Donkey to himself. "I must not move about too much nor let any of the other toys rub against me until I am quite dry. If they did they would blur or scratch my shiny varnish coat, and that would be too bad. But after I am dry I'll have some fun. Just wait until to-night! Then there will be some great times in this workshop of Santa Claus!"

The reason the Nodding Donkey said this, was because at night, when Santa Claus and his merry helpers had gone, the toys were allowed to do as they pleased. They could make believe come to life, and move about, having all sorts of adventures.

But, presto! the moment daylight came, or any one looked at them, the toys became as straight and stiff and motionless as any toys that are in your playroom. For all you know some of your toys may move about and pretend to come to life when you are asleep. But it is of no use for you to stay awake, watching to see if they will, for as long as any eyes are peeping, or ears are listening, the toys will never do anything of themselves.

The Nodding Donkey knew that when Santa Claus and the workers were gone he and the other toys could do as they pleased, and he could hardly wait for that time to come.

"But while I am waiting I will stay here on the shelf and get hard and dry," said the Nodding Donkey to himself.

Once more he looked in the glass on the doll's bureau, and he was well pleased with himself, was the Nodding Donkey.

Such a busy place was the workshop of Santa Claus at the North Pole, where the Nodding Donkey was drying in his coat of varnish!

The place was like a great big greenhouse, all made of glass, only the glass was sheets of crystal-clear ice. Santa Claus needed plenty of light in his workshop, for in the dark it is not easy to put red cheeks and blue eyes on dolls, or paint toy soldiers and wind up the springs of the toys that move.

The workshop of Santa Claus, then, was like a big greenhouse, only no flowers grew in it because it is very cold at the North Pole. All about was snow and ice, but Santa Claus did not mind the cold, nor did his workmen, for they were dressed in fur, like the polar bears and the seals.

On each side of the big shop, with its icy glass roof, were work benches. At these benches sat the funny little men who made the toys.

Some were stuffing sawdust into dolls, others were putting the lids on the boxes where the Jacks lived, and still others were trying the Jumping Jacks to see that they jerked their legs and arms properly.

Up and down, between the rows of benches, walked Santa Claus himself. Now and then some workman would call:

"Please look here, Santa Claus! Shall I make this Tin Soldier with a sword or a gun?"

And St. Nicholas would answer:

"That Soldier needs a sword. He is going to be a Captain."

Then another little man would call, from the other side of the shop:

"Here is a Calico Clown who doesn't squeak when I press on his stomach. Something must be wrong with him, Santa Claus."

Then Santa Claus would put on his glasses, stroke his long, white beard and look at the Calico Clown.

"Humph! I should say he wouldn't squeak!" the old gentleman would remark. "You have his squeaker in upside down! That would never do for some little boy or girl to find on Christmas morning! Take the squeaker out and put it in right."

"How careless of me!" the little workman would exclaim. And then Santa Claus and the other workmen would laugh, for this workshop was the jolliest place in the world, and the man would fix the Calico Clown right.

"I'm glad I was born in this place," said the Nodding Donkey to himself, as his head swayed to and fro. "This is really the first day of my life. I wish night would come, so I could move about and talk to the other toys. I wonder how long I shall have to wait?"

Not far from the doll's bureau, which held the looking glass, was a toy house, and in it was a toy clock. The Donkey looked in through the window of the toy house and saw the toy clock. The hands pointed to four o'clock.

"The men stop work at five," thought the Donkey. "After that it will be dark and I can move about—that is if my varnish is dry."

Santa Claus was walking up and down between the rows of work benches. The dear old gentleman was pulling his beard and smiling.

"Come, my merry men!" he called in his jolly voice, "you must work a little faster. It is nearly five, when it will be time to stop for the day, and it is so near Christmas that I fear we shall never get enough toys made. So hurry all you can!"

"We will, Santa Claus," the men answered. And the one who had made the Nodding Donkey asked:

"When are you going to take a load of toys down to Earth?"

"The first thing in the morning," was the answer. "Many of the stores have written me, asking me to hurry some toys to them. I shall hitch up my reindeer to the sleigh and take a big bag of toys down to Earth to-morrow. So get ready for me as many as you can.

"Yes," went on Santa Claus, and he looked right at the Nodding Donkey, "I must take a big bag of toys to Earth to-morrow, as soon as it is daylight. So hurry, my merry men!"

And the workmen hurried as fast as they could.

Ting! suddenly struck the big clock in the workshop. And ting! went the little toy clock in the toy house.

"Time to stop for supper!" called Santa Claus, and all the little men laid aside the toys on which they were working. Then such a bustle and hustle there was to get out of the shop; for the day had come to an end.

Night settled down over North Pole Land. It was dark, but in the house where Santa Claus lived with his men some Japanese lanterns, hung from icicles, gave them light to see to eat their supper.

In the toy shop it was just dimly light, for one lantern had been left burning there, in case Santa Claus might want to go in after hours to see if everything was all right.

And by the light of this one lamp the Nodding Donkey saw a curious sight. Over on his left the Plush Bear raised one paw and scratched his nose. On the Donkey's right the China Cat opened her china mouth and softly said:

"Mew!"

And then, on the next shelf, a Rolling Elephant, who could wheel about, spoke through his trunk, and said:

"The time has come for us to have some fun, my friends!"

"Right you are!" mewed the China Cat.

"And we have a new toy with us," said the Plush Bear. "Would you like to play with us?" he asked the Nodding Donkey.

The Nodding Donkey moved his head up and down to say "yes," for he was afraid of speaking aloud, lest he might wrinkle his new varnish.

"All right, now for some jolly times!" said the Rolling Elephant, and he began to climb down from the shelf, using his trunk as well as his legs.

"Ouch! Look out there! You're stretching my neck!" suddenly cried a Spotted Wooden Giraffe, and the Nodding Donkey, looking up, saw that the Elephant had wound his trunk around the long neck of the Giraffe.

"Oh, I'm going to fall! Catch me, somebody!" cried the Spotted Giraffe. "Oh, if I fall off the shelf I'll be broken to bits! Will no one save me?"

CHAPTER II

A WONDERFUL VOYAGE

"Goodness me! this is a lot of excitement for one who has just come to life and had his first coat of varnish!" thought the Nodding Donkey as he saw what seemed to be a sad accident about to happen. "I wonder if I could do anything to help save the Spotted Giraffe? I must try to do all I can. It will be the first time I have ever moved all by myself."

"Stand aside, if you please! I'll save the Spotted Giraffe!" suddenly called a voice, and from a shelf just underneath the one from which the Rolling Elephant had pulled the long-necked creature there stepped a Jolly Fisherman. This toy fisherman had a large net for catching crabs or lobsters, and he held it out for the Spotted Giraffe to fall into.

Down the Giraffe fell, but he landed in the net of the Jolly Fisherman, just as a circus performer falls into a net from a high trapeze, and he was not harmed.

"Dear! I'm glad you caught me," said the Giraffe, after he had managed to climb out of the net to the top of a work table which ran under all the shelves.

"Yes, I got there just in time," replied the Jolly Fisherman, as he slung his net over his shoulder again.

"And I'm very sorry I pulled you from the shelf," said the Rolling Elephant. "I didn't mean to do it, Mr. Giraffe."

"Well, as long as no harm is done, we'll forget all about it and have some fun," put in the Plush Bear. "This doesn't happen every night," the Bear went on, speaking to the Nodding Donkey. "You must not get the idea that it is dangerous here."

"Oh, no, I think it's a very nice place," the Nodding Donkey answered. "It's my first day here, you see."

"Oh, yes, it's easy to see that," said the China Cat. "You are so new and shiny any one would know you were just made. Well, now what shall we do? Who has a game to suggest or a riddle to ask?" and, as she spoke, she put out her paw and began to roll a red rubber ball on the shelf near her. For, though she was very stiff in the daytime, being made of china like a dinner plate, the Cat could easily move about at night if no human eyes watched her.

"Let's play a guessing game," suggested the Rolling Elephant, who, by this time had managed to get down to the table without upsetting any more of the toys. "If we play tag or hide and go seek, I'm so big and clumsy I may knock over something and break it."

"That's so—you might," growled the Plush Bear, but, though he spoke in a growling voice he was not at all cross. It was just his way of talking. "Well, what sort of a guessing game do you want to play, Mr. Elephant?"

"I'll think of something, and you must all see if you can guess what it is."

"That's too hard a game," objected the China Cat. "There are so many things you might think of."

"Well, I'll give you a little help," returned the Rolling Elephant. "I'm thinking of something that goes up and down and also sideways."

For a moment none of the toys spoke. Then, all of a sudden, the Plush Bear cried:

"You're thinking of the Nodding Donkey! His head goes up and down and also sideways."

"That's right!" admitted the Rolling Elephant. "I didn't imagine you'd guess so soon. Now it's your turn to think of something."

"Let's have the Nodding Donkey give the next question," suggested the China Cat. "It's his birthday, you know, and we ought to help him remember it."

"Go ahead! Give us something to guess, Nodding Donkey!" growled the Plush Bear.

"Let me think," said the new toy, slowly. "Ah, I have it! What am I thinking of that is like a snowball and has two eyes?"

"A snowman!" guessed a wax doll.

"No," said the Nodding Donkey, laughing.

"A Polar Bear," suggested the Rolling Elephant.

"No," said the Donkey again.

Then the toys thought very hard.

"Is it a rubber doll?" asked a Jack in the Box. "No, it couldn't be that," he went on, "for a rubber doll isn't as white as a snowball. I give up!"

"But I don't!" suddenly cried a Tin Soldier. "You were thinking of our White China Cat, weren't you?" he asked.

"Yes," answered the Nodding Donkey, "I was. You have guessed it!"

"Now it's the Tin Soldier's turn to give us something to guess," said the Elephant. "Oh, we're having lots of fun!"

And so the toys were. All through the night they played about in the North Pole workshop of Santa Claus. When it was nearly morning the Nodding Donkey spoke to the Plush Bear, asking:

"Where is this Earth place, that Santa Claus said he was going to take some of us?"

"Oh, my! don't ask me," said the Plush Bear. "I've never been down to Earth, though I know packs and packs of toys have been taken there. But it must be a real jolly sort of place, for every time Santa Claus goes there he comes back laughing and seems very happy. Then he loads up some more toys to take there."

"I think I should like to go," murmured the Nodding Donkey. "How does one go—in one of the toy trains of cars I see on the shelves?"

"Oh, my, no!" laughed the Plush Bear. "Santa Claus takes the toys to Earth in his sleigh, drawn by reindeer."

"Oh, how wonderful!" brayed the Donkey. "I wonder if I shall soon take that wonderful voyage. I hope I may!"

"Hush!" suddenly called the Rolling Elephant. "Santa Claus and the workmen are coming in and they must not see us at our make-believe play. Quick! To your shelves, all of you!"

Such a scramble as there was on the part of the toys! Some helped the others to climb up, and just as the last of them, including the Nodding Donkey, were safely in place, the door of the shop opened and in came Santa Claus and his men.

Then such a bustling about as there was! And from outside the shop could be heard the jingle of bells.

"Those must be the reindeer," thought the Nodding Donkey. "Oh, what a jolly time I shall have if I ride in the sleigh with Santa Claus!"

Never was there such a busy time in the shop of Santa Claus! Jolly St. Nicholas himself hurried here and there, helping his men pick up different toys which were put in a big bag. One of the men stopped in front of the Nodding Donkey.

"Shall I put this chap in, Santa Claus?" the man inquired.

"Is the varnish dry?" asked St. Nicholas.

"Yes," answered the little man, testing it lightly with his finger.

"Then put him in," said Santa Claus. "I'll take the Nodding Donkey to Earth with me."

"Oh, joy! Now I shall have some adventures! Now I shall see what the Earth is like!" thought the Nodding Donkey.

A moment later he was picked up, wrapped in soft paper, and thrust into a bag.

"Oh, how very dark it is here," said the Donkey in a whisper.

"Hush!" whispered a Jumping Jack near him. "Don't talk! Santa Claus might hear you. He has very sharp ears. You'll be all right. It is no darker than night."

More toys, all carefully wrapped, came tumbling into the bag, and the merry jingle of bells grew louder. Then the voice of Santa Claus could be heard shouting:

"Hi there, Dasher! Stand still, Prancer! Whoa, Blitzen! What's the matter, Comet? Are you anxious to get to Earth again? Well, we'll soon start. Steady there, Cupid! Whoa!"

"He's talking to his reindeer," whispered the Jumping Jack.

Suddenly the toys in the big sack felt themselves being picked up. Santa Claus had slung them over his back to carry out to the sleigh. A moment later the Nodding Donkey felt a breath of cold air strike him, but he did not mind, as he had on a warm coat of varnish.

Up and down, and from side to side the toys in the bag felt themselves being jostled, until they were set down in the big sleigh.

"All aboard!" called Santa Claus, as he took his seat and gathered up the reins. "Come, Dasher! On, Prancer! Hi, Donner and Blitzen! Down to Earth you go with the Christmas toys!"

There was another jolly jingle of bells, and the toys felt themselves being whisked away over the snow. There was a little hole in the bag near the Nodding Donkey, and also a hole in the paper in which he was wrapped. He could look out, and on every side he saw big piles of snow. Snow was also falling from the clouds.

On and on rushed the sleigh of Santa Claus, drawn by the eight reindeer. Over the clouds and drifts of snow, and through the white flakes they rushed, the sleigh-bells playing a merry tune.

"Oh, this is a wonderful voyage!" thought the Nodding Donkey. "I wonder when I shall reach the Earth?"

Suddenly there was a hard shock. The sleigh stopped as Santa Claus shouted, and then, all at once, the Nodding Donkey felt himself shooting out of the hole in the bag. Into a deep snowdrift he fell, and there he stuck, head down and feet up in the air!

12

CHAPTER III

THE JOLLY STORE

"Dear me," thought the Nodding Donkey to himself, as he felt the cold, chilly snow all about him, "this is most dreadful! I hope Santa Claus has not become angry with me and sent me back to the North Pole. I did so much want to go down to Earth and be in a big store for Christmas. I hope I'm not back at the North Pole."

The Nodding Donkey said this aloud, and, as he spoke, he wobbled his head from side to side and tried to turn over so he could stand on his feet.

"Here! Don't do that!" suddenly whispered a voice in one of the Donkey's large ears. "Don't you know it isn't allowed for you to move when any one is looking at you?"

"I didn't know any one was looking at me," the Nodding Donkey answered. "I thought Santa Claus had tossed me back to the North Pole."

"Hush! No! Nothing like that has happened," the voice went on, and, by turning his loose head to one side, the Nodding Donkey saw that a large Jumping Jack was whispering to him.

"There has been an accident," went on the Jumping Jack. "The sleigh of Santa Claus banged into a hard, frozen snow cloud, and we were thrown out into a snowdrift. I am not hurt, and I hope you are not. But we must not talk or move much more, for I see Santa Claus coming this way, and even he is not allowed to see us pretend to be alive, so that we move and talk. He is coming to pick us up, I guess."

And then both toys had to keep quiet, for Santa Claus came stalking along in his big leather boots. St. Nicholas was wiping some snowflakes out of his eyes, his breath made clouds of steam in the frosty air and his cheeks were as red as the reddest apple you ever saw.

"Oh, ho! Here are some of my toys!" cried the jolly old gentleman as he saw the Nodding Donkey and the Jumping Jack. "I was afraid I had lost you. We nearly had a bad accident," he went on, speaking to himself, but loudly enough for the Nodding Donkey to hear. "My reindeer got off the road and ran into a snow cloud and the sleigh was upset."

"It's just as the Jumping Jack told me," thought the Nodding Donkey.

"Steady there, Comet! Keep quiet, Prancer!" called St. Nicholas to his animals, who, stamping their legs, made the bells jingle. "We shall soon be on our way again. Nothing is broken."

Santa Claus picked up the Donkey and the Jumping Jack and carried them back to the sleigh. There the two toys could see their friends, some lying on the seat of the sleigh and others resting in the big bag, through the hole of which the Nodding Donkey had slipped out, falling into the snow.

"Ha! I must fix that hole in the bag," cried Santa Claus, as he noticed it.

St. Nicholas tied some string around the hole in the sack, and then, having again wrapped the tissue paper around the Donkey, the Jumping Jack, and the other toys that had fallen out, the red-cheeked old gentleman put them in the bag and fastened it shut.

"Now we're off again!" cried Santa Claus, as he took his seat in the sleigh. "Trot along, Comet! Fly away, Prancer! Lively there, Donner and Blitzen! We must get down to Earth with these toys, and then back again to North Pole Land for another load! Trot along, my speedy reindeer!"

The reindeer shook their heads, which made the bells jingle more merrily than before, they stamped their feet on the hard, frozen road that led from the North Pole to Earth, and then away they darted. Santa Claus drove them carefully, steering away from snow clouds, and soon the motion was so swift and smooth that the Nodding Donkey went to sleep, and so did most of the other toys in the big sack.

And what a funny dream the Nodding Donkey had! He imagined that he was tumbling around a feather bed and that a Blue Dog was chasing him with a yellow feather duster.

"Don't tickle me with that feather duster!" he thought he cried.

"I won't if you'll sing a song through your ears," said the Blue Dog.

"I can't sing through my ears," wailed the Nodding Donkey, and then of a sudden he seemed to roll over and the dog and the feather bed came down on top of him. Then he seemed to give a sneeze and that blew the dog away and sent the feathers of the bed out into one big snowstorm!

It was dark when the Nodding Donkey awoke. He did not hear the jingle of the bells, nor could he feel the sleigh being drawn along by the reindeer. He could see nothing, either, for it was very black and dark. But he heard some voices talking, and one he knew was that of Santa Claus.

"Now I have brought you a whole sleighful of toys," said St. Nicholas.

"Yes, and I am glad to get them," another voice answered. "The stores are almost empty and it is near Christmas time. I shall send a lot of the toys to the stores the first thing in the morning."

Santa Claus had arrived, in the night, at a large warehouse, where boxes, bales and bags of toys were kept until they could be sent around to the different stores. The Nodding Donkey, the Jumping Jack and the others felt themselves being lifted out of the bag and placed on the floor or on shelves. But they could see nothing, for Santa Claus always comes to Earth in the darkness, so no one sees him. And it was the Earth that the toys had now reached.

"Dear me, this isn't much fun!" complained the Nodding Donkey, as he stood on a shelf in the darkness. Faint and far off he could hear the bells of Santa Claus' reindeer jingling as jolly St. Nicholas drove back to North Pole Land. "I thought the Earth was such a wonderful place," went on the Nodding Donkey. "But I don't like it here at all."

"Hush!" begged the Jumping Jack. "It is night. You have seen nothing yet. Wait until morning."

And, after a while, streaks of light began to come in through the windows of the warehouse where the toys had been left. The sun was rising. From a window near him the Nodding Donkey caught a glimpse of snow outside, but the land was very different from the North Pole where he had been made.

The Nodding Donkey was turning his head to speak to the Jumping Jack, and he was going to take a look and see what other toys were near him, when, all of a sudden, three or four men came into the room. They had hammers, nails and boards in their hands.

"Hurry now!" cried one of the men. "We must box up a lot of these toys and send them to the different stores. It will be Christmas before we know it."

Suddenly one of the men caught hold of the Nodding Donkey, and also of a large doll that had been on the same shelf.

"I'll pack these in a box," said the man. "I just need them to fill one corner. Then I'll ship them off."

The Nodding Donkey wished his friend the Jumping Jack might go in the same box with him, but it was not to be. The Donkey gave one last look at his companion of the snowdrift, and a moment later he was being wrapped in tissue paper again, and was packed down in a corner of a large box. The doll was treated the same way.

Then the board cover was put on the box, and nailed shut with a loud hammering noise.

"Dear me, in the dark again!" said the Nodding Donkey. "I don't seem to be having a good time at all."

"Never mind! It will not last long," said the Doll, who was made of cloth, so it did not matter how much she was squeezed. "We will soon be in the light again."

The toys in the box could hear loud talking going on in the warehouse where they had been left by Santa Claus. They could also hear men moving about and the bang and rattle of boxes, like theirs, as the cases were nailed up and taken away.

Finally the Nodding Donkey, the doll, and other toys who were packed together, felt their box being tilted up on one end. By this time the Nodding Donkey was getting used to being stood on his head, or turned over on his back, and he did not mind it.

"Hurry up! Load this box on a truck and take it to the Mugg store!" cried a voice.

"The Mugg store! I wonder where that is!" thought the Nodding Donkey.

And then he felt the box in which he lay being lifted up and carried along. There were bumps, thumps, turnings and twistings, and then the Nodding Donkey felt himself gliding along.

But he soon noticed that this ride was not as smooth as had been the one from North Pole Land to the Earth. Instead of riding in a sleigh drawn by reindeer, the Nodding Donkey was riding on an automobile truck, and as it went out in the street it bumped and rattled along.

There was so much noise and confusion, and it was so warm and cosy in the box where he was packed, that, before he knew it, the Nodding Donkey had fallen asleep. And, as he slept, the Nodding Donkey dreamed.

He dreamed that he was back in the workshop of Santa Claus at the North Pole and on a shelf with other toys. Suddenly a Wooden Soldier began beating on the Donkey's back with the end of a gun.

"Rub-a-dub-dub!" drummed the Soldier, and the Donkey's head nodded so hard that he feared it would be shaken off.

"Stop! Stop!" cried the Donkey in his dream, and then he suddenly awakened. He heard a hammering, but it was not on his back. It was outside the case in which he was packed, and he soon noticed that some one was knocking off the boards that formed the cover.

With a wrench and a squeak one of the cover boards was raised, letting in a flood of light. The Nodding Donkey blinked his eyes, coming out of the darkness into the glare of the light. Then he felt himself being lifted up and set on a shelf. At the same time he heard a pleasant voice saying:

"Here is the case of new toys, Daughters. And see, one of the very newest is a Nodding Donkey! I'm sure he will please some little boy or girl!"

The Nodding Donkey looked around him. He was on a shelf in the jolliest toy store he had ever imagined. It was almost as nice as the workshop of Santa Claus. Standing in front of the shelf was a white-haired old man and two ladies, one on either side of him. The three were looking at the Nodding Donkey, who bowed his head at them as if saying:

"How do you do? I am very glad to meet you!"

CHAPTER IV

THE CHINA CAT

The Nodding Donkey stood straight and stiff on his four legs, with his shiny, new coat of varnish—the one he had received in the workshop of Santa Claus at the North Pole. The Donkey wished he might move about and talk with some of the other toys he saw all around him, but he dared not, as the old gentleman and the two ladies were standing in front of him and looking straight at the toy. All the Donkey dared do was to nod his head, for, being made on purpose to do that, it was perfectly proper for him to do so, just as the Jumping Jack jumped, or some of the funny Clowns banged together their brass cymbals.

"Isn't he the dearest Donkey you ever saw, Angelina?" said one of the ladies to the other.

"He certainly is, Geraldine," was the answer. "But something seems to be the matter with his head. It is loose!"

"Tut! Tut! Nonsense! It is made that way, just the same as the moving head of the Fuzzy Bear," said the old gentleman, whose name was Horatio Mugg. At first the Nodding Donkey had taken this old gentleman for a relative of Santa Claus, for he had the same white hair and whiskers and wore almost the same sort of glasses. But a second look showed the Nodding Donkey that this was not any relation of St. Nicholas. Besides, this toy store was not at all like the workshop of Santa Claus.

The Nodding Donkey was at last on Earth in a toy store, and there, it was hoped, some one would see him and buy him for some boy or girl for Christmas.

The toy store was kept by Mr. Horatio Mugg and his two daughters, one being named Angelina and the other Geraldine.

Mr. Horatio Mugg was the jolliest toy-store man you can imagine! Since his own two daughters had grown up he seemed to think he must look after all the other children in his neighborhood. He was always glad to see the boys and girls in his store. He liked to have them look at the toys, and sometimes he showed them how steam engines or flying machines worked.

Of course there were many dolls, big and little—Sawdust Dolls, Bisque Dolls, Wooden Dolls, some very handsomely dressed, with silk or satin dresses and white stockings and white kid shoes. And some had the cutest hats, and some even had gloves, think of that!

And then the animals—Lions and Tigers, and a Striped Zebra, and funny Monkeys and Goats, Dogs, Spotted Cows and many kinds of Rocking

Horses. And even funny little Mice, that ran all around the floor when they were wound up.

And then the other toys—trains of cars, fire engines, building blocks, and oh! so many, many things! It was truly a wonderful place, was that store. It was a place where you could spend an hour or two and the time would fly so fast you would scarcely know where it had gone to.

Mr. Mugg knew all about toys, which kind were the best for boys, which the girls liked the best, and he knew which to put in his window so the children would stop and press their noses flat against the glass to look and see the playthings.

"Yes, the Nodding Donkey will be a fine toy for Christmas," said Mr. Mugg, looking over the tops of his glasses at the new arrival. "This last box of playthings I received are the best we ever had. Santa Claus and his men certainly are preparing a fine Christmas this year."

"I think I shall dust off the Donkey," said Geraldine. "He will be much shinier then, and look better."

"And I must dust the China Cat," said her sister Angelina. "She is so white that the least speck shows on her. Real white cats are very fussy about keeping themselves clean, so I do not see why a white China Cat should not be treated the same way. You dust the Nodding Donkey, Geraldine, and I'll dust the Cat."

"That China Cat seems to act as if she wanted to speak to me," thought the Donkey. "Perhaps, after the store is closed to-night, as the workshop of Santa Claus is closed, I may speak to her."

Up and down and to and fro the head of the Nodding Donkey moved as Geraldine Mugg dusted him. Then she set him back on the shelf, as her sister did the China Cat.

"Come here, Daughters, and see this set of Soldiers," called Mr. Mugg, who was unpacking more toys from the box. "They are the nicest we ever had."

"Oh, what fine red coats they wear!" said Angelina.

"And how their guns shine!" exclaimed Geraldine. "Our store will look lovely when we get all the toys placed in it."

"I think the store looks very well as it is," thought the Nodding Donkey to himself, as he stood straight and stiff on his shelf, his coat of varnish glistening in the light. "I never saw such a wonderful place."

And, indeed, the toy store of Mr. Horatio Mugg was a place of delight for all boys and girls. I could not begin to tell you all the things that were in it. Mr.

Mugg kept only toys. All the different sorts that were ever made were there gathered together, ready for the Christmas trade.

And as the Nodding Donkey, standing beside the white China Cat, looked on and listened, he saw boys and girls, with their fathers or mothers, coming in to look at the toys. Some were ordered to be put away until Christmas should come. Others were taken at once, to be mailed perhaps to some far-off city.

As the Nodding Donkey watched he saw a little boy with blue eyes and golden hair come in and point to a Jack in the Box.

"Please, Mother, will you tell Santa Claus to bring me that for Christmas?" begged the little boy.

"Yes, I will do that," his mother promised. "And now, Sister, what would you like?" the lady asked.

The Nodding Donkey looked down and saw a little girl, with dark hair and brown eyes standing beside the little boy. This girl pointed to a large doll, and, to his surprise, the Donkey saw that it was the same one he had spoken to in the packing case.

"You may put that Doll aside for my little girl for Christmas, Mr. Mugg," said the lady.

"Very well, Madam, it shall be done," replied the toy man, and he lifted the Cloth Doll down off the shelf.

"Oh, dear! she is going away, and I shall never see her again," thought the Nodding Donkey. "That is the only sad part of life for us toys. We make friends, but we never know how long we may keep them. We are so often separated."

Mr. Mugg put the doll down under the counter, where no other little girl might see her and want her. Then the toy man reached up and gently touched the head of the Donkey, so that it nodded harder than ever.

"Here is a new toy that just came in," said Mr. Mugg. "It is one of the latest. It is called a Nodding Donkey, and once you start his head going it will move for hours."

"Oh, it is nice!" said the lady. "Would you rather have that than your Jack in the Box, Robert?" she asked the little boy.

The boy stood first on one foot and then on the other. He looked first at the Jack in the Box and then at the Donkey.

"They are both nice," he said; "but I think I would rather have the Jack. I'll have the Donkey next Christmas."

The Jack in the Box was set aside with the Cloth Doll, and then the lady and the little boy and girl passed on. But all that day there were many other boys and girls who came into the store to look at the toys. Some only came to look, while others, as before, bought the things they wanted, or had them set aside for Christmas.

After a while it began to grow dark in the store, just as it had grown dark in the workshop of Santa Claus.

"Now I will soon be able to move about and talk to the other toys," thought the Nodding Donkey. But this was not to be—just yet.

"Turn on the lights, Angelina," called Mr. Mugg to his daughter, and soon the store was glowing brightly.

"Hum! It seems they work at night here, as well as by day," thought the Nodding Donkey. "It was not so at North Pole Land. But it is very jolly, and I like it."

During the evening, when the lights were glowing, many other customers came in, but there were not so many boys and girls. The Nodding Donkey had been taken down more than once and made to do his trick of shaking his head, but, so far, no one had bought him. And though the China Cat had also been looked at and admired, no one had bought her.

At last Mr. Mugg stretched his arms, yawned as though he might be very sleepy, and said:

"Turn out the lights, Angelina! It is time to close the shop and go to bed."

Soon the toy shop was in darkness, all except one light that was kept burning all night. The place became very still and quiet, the only noise being made by a little mouse, who came out to get some crumbs dropped by Mr. Mugg, who had eaten his lunch in the store.

"Ahem!" suddenly said the Nodding Donkey. "Do you mind if I speak to you?" he asked the China Cat, who stood near him on the shelf.

"Not at all," was the kind answer. "I was just going to ask how you came here."

"I came direct from the workshop of Santa Claus at the North Pole," answered the Nodding Donkey. "And I suppose, just as we toys could do there, that we are allowed to move about and talk while here."

"Oh, yes," answered the China Cat. "We can make believe we are alive as long as no one sees us. But tell me, how is everything at the North Pole? It is some time since I was there, as I was made early in the season."

"Well, Santa Claus is as happy and jolly as ever," said the Nodding Donkey, "and his men are just as busy. We had a dreadful accident though, coming down to Earth!"

"You did?" mewed the China Cat. "Tell me about it," and she moved her tail from one side to the other.

Before the Nodding Donkey could speak in answer to this request, a voice suddenly asked:

"I say, Nodding Donkey, do you kick?"

"Kick? Of course not," the Nodding Donkey answered. "Why do you ask such a question? Who are you, anyhow?" and he looked all around.

"Hush! Don't get him started," whispered the China Cat. "It's the Policeman with his club, and if he begins to tickle you he'll never stop. Oh, here he comes now! Here comes the Policeman!"

CHAPTER V

THE LAME BOY

When the China Cat said: "Here comes the Policeman!" the Nodding Donkey, who did not know just what a policeman was, was quite curious to see who was coming. So he walked to the edge of the shelf and bent his head as far down as he could in order to see.

"Be careful! You might fall!" mewed the China Cat.

"Ha! If he falls, then I'll pick him up! That's what I'm here for, to help in case of accident. I could ring for the ambulance!" suddenly came in the same voice that had asked if the Nodding Donkey kicked.

"On second thought perhaps it will be just as well to have an accident. It will give us something to talk about," the voice went on. "Go ahead, Nodding Donkey. Fall off the shelf. I'll pick you up and send you to the toy hospital in the toy ambulance with the clanging bell."

"Indeed I am not going to fall!" brayed the Donkey. "Who is he, anyhow?" he whispered to the China Cat.

"That's the Policeman I was telling you about," was the answer. "Here he comes now!"

And suddenly the Policeman's voice went on, saying:

"Come now! Move along! Don't block up the sidewalk! Move on! Don't loiter here!"

The Nodding Donkey looked to one side and there he saw a toy Policeman, dressed just as a real one would be, with blue coat, brass buttons, a white helmet and a club that swung on the end of a leather string. The Policeman walked along, for he could do that when a spring inside him was wound up. And as he walked he swung his club to and fro, and said, just like a real policeman:

"Come now, move along! Don't block up the sidewalk." Then he added, in a different tone: "There is no accident now, but if that Nodding Donkey would only fall off the shelf we might have one."

"Indeed, and I'm not going to fall off the shelf just for fun!" brayed the Donkey.

"Oh, aren't you? Then we must make fun in some other way," said the toy Policeman. "How are you feeling?" and with that he jumped up on the shelf beside the Donkey and tickled him in the ribs with the club.

"Oh, don't do—ha! ha!—Don't—ha! ha!—do that!" laughed the Donkey. "You make me feel so funny I may fall!"

The Nodding Donkey is Tickled by the Toy Policeman. The Nodding Donkey is Tickled by the Toy Policeman.

Page 50

"Well, if you do, I'll pick you up," said the Policeman, and he twisted his club around on the Donkey's ribs in such a funny way that the nodding creature laughed "ha! ha!" and "ho! ho!"

"I thought I'd stir things up and make them rather lively!" said the Policeman, with a jolly grin on his red face. "How are you feeling?" he asked, turning to the China Cat.

"I feel quite good enough without having you tickle me," she answered, as she got up to move away.

"Oh, you'll feel ever so much better after I tickle you!" cried the Policeman, and he reached out his club toward the Cat. But he was not quick enough. She slipped behind a Jack in the Box, where the Policeman could not see her.

"Well, I guess I'll tickle you again," said the toy with the club, as he turned back toward the Nodding Donkey.

"Oh, no, don't, please!" begged the long-eared chap. "I've had quite enough. When you tickle me I laugh, and when I laugh my head nods harder than it ought to, and maybe it might nod off."

"Oh, I wouldn't want that to happen!" exclaimed the Policeman. "That would be too bad an accident. I guess I'll walk down the shelf and see if there's a fire anywhere," he went on, and away he stalked, swinging his club from side to side.

"Oh, I hope there isn't a fire here," said the Nodding Donkey, as the China Cat came out from behind the Jack's box. "I am not used to being hot. I came from the cold North Pole."

"No, there isn't any fire. If there were you would soon see the toy Fireman and the Fire Engine starting out," replied the China Cat. "I don't like fires myself, and I detest the water they squirt on them. We cats don't like water, you know."

"So I have heard," said the Nodding Donkey.

"Dear me! there's a speck of dirt on my tail," suddenly mewed the China Cat, and she leaned over, and with her red tongue washed her tail clean.

Meanwhile the Policeman walked on down the counter, as though it were a street, and he swung his club and said:

"Move on now! Don't crowd the sidewalk! Everybody must keep moving!"

"Isn't he funny?" asked the Nodding Donkey.

"He is when he doesn't tickle you," said the China Cat, as she looked in a Doll's mirror to see if she had any more specks of dirt on her white coat. But she was nice and clean, was the China Cat.

Then the toys in the store of Horatio Mugg began to have lots of fun. They told stories, sang songs, made up riddles for one another to guess and played tag and hide-and-go-seek. They were allowed to do all this because it was night and no one was watching them. But as soon as daylight came and Mr. Mugg or Miss Angelina or Miss Geraldine or any of the customers came into the store, the toys must be very still and quiet.

"Is this the only store you were ever in?" asked the Donkey of the Cat, as they sat near each other after a lively game of tag.

"No, I was in one other," was the answer. "It was a store in which there lived a Sawdust Doll, a Lamb on Wheels, a Monkey on a Stick and many other playthings."

"Why did you leave?" asked the Donkey. "Was it because there were no other cats there for you to mew to?"

"No, it was not that," was the answer.

"Then why did you leave?" asked the Nodding Donkey.

"Well, one Christmas I was bought by a gentleman who sent me to a lady," was the answer. "She was a lady who was always changing things that came to her from the store. She would buy a thing one day and change it, or send it back, the next.

"And when I came to her as a Christmas present, she happened to have a little China Dog. I guess she thought the dog might bark at me. Anyhow, she sent me back to the store, only she sent me here instead of to the store where the Calico Clown and the other toys lived, and the mistake was never found out. Mr. Mugg and his daughters took me in, and I have been here ever since."

"Do you ever see your friend, the Monkey on a Stick, or hear from the Sawdust Doll?" asked the Donkey.

"Once in a while," was the answer. "Sometimes, when the grown folk buy toys for children they pick out the wrong ones, and the toys are brought back or exchanged. These toys that come back tell us of the houses where they have spent a few days.

"Once a Jumping Jack who was brought back in this way told about being in a house where the Sawdust Doll lived, and where there was also a White Rocking Horse I used to know."

"I should like to meet the White Rocking Horse," said the Nodding Donkey. "He might be a distant relation of mine."

"Perhaps," agreed the China Cat. "But now I think it is time we got back on our shelves. I see daylight beginning to peep in the window, and it would never do for Mr. Mugg or Miss Angelina or Miss Geraldine to see us moving about."

"I suppose not," said the Nodding Donkey, somewhat sadly.

"Move along, everybody! Move back to your places! Daylight is coming!" called the Policeman, as he walked past swinging his club.

And, a little later, when all the toys were back on the shelves, the sun rose, and in came Mr. Mugg to open the store for the day.

All that day people came and went in the toy store, some coming to look, and others to buy. Some of the toys were taken away, and the Nodding Donkey wondered when it would be his turn. But, though he was often taken up, shown and admired, no one purchased him.

"I know what I will do, so that Donkey will be sold!" said Mr. Mugg in the afternoon.

"What?" asked Miss Angelina.

"I will put him in the show window," answered her father.

"Oh, let me decorate the show window!" begged Miss Geraldine. "I'll make up a scene with a Christmas tree, and put the Nodding Donkey under it."

"Very well," agreed Mr. Mugg. "I will leave the show window to you, Geraldine. Make it look as pretty as you can."

And Miss Geraldine did. She got a little Christmas tree and set it up in a box. Then she put some tiny electric lights on it, and also some toys. Other toys were put under the tree, and one of these was the Nodding Donkey.

"Oh, now I can see things!" said the Donkey to himself, as he found he could look right out into the street. It was a scene he had never observed before. All his life had been spent in the workshop of Santa Claus or in the toy store. He was most delighted to look out into the street.

It was snowing, and crowds were hurrying to and fro, doing their Christmas shopping. After the show window in the store of Mr. Horatio Mugg had been newly decorated by Miss Geraldine, many boys and girls and grown folk, too, stopped to peer in. They looked at the Nodding Donkey, at the Jumping Jacks, at the Dolls, the toy Fire Engines, at the Soldiers and at the Policeman.

Toward evening, when the lights had just been set aglow, the Nodding Donkey saw, coming toward the window, a little lame boy. He had to walk on crutches, and with him was a lady who had hold of his arm.

"Oh, Mother, look at the new toys!" cried the lame boy. "And see that Donkey! Why, he's shaking his head at me! Look, he's making his head go up and down! I guess he thinks I asked you if you'd buy him for me, and he's saying 'yes'; isn't he, Mother?"

"Perhaps," answered the lady. "Would you like that Nodding Donkey for Christmas, Joe?"

"Oh, I just would!" cried the lame boy. "Let's go in and look at him. Maybe I can hold him in my hands! Oh, I'd just love that Nodding Donkey!"

CHAPTER VI

A NEW HOME

For a minute or two longer the lame boy and his mother stood in front of the show window of the toy shop of Mr. Horatio Mugg and his two daughters. The lame boy looked at the Nodding Donkey and the Nodding Donkey bobbed his head in such a funny fashion that the lame boy smiled.

"I'm glad I could make him do that," thought the Donkey. "He doesn't look so sad when he smiles. I wonder what is the matter with him that he walks in such a funny way?"

Of course the Nodding Donkey did not know what it meant to be lame. His own wooden legs were straight and stiff, and he did not need crutches, as did the lame boy.

"Be sure it is the Nodding Donkey you want, and not some other toy," said the boy's mother, as they looked at the things in the window.

"Yes, Mother, I'd rather have him than anything else," the boy answered, and into the store they went. Mr. Mugg came out from behind the counter.

"Would you like to look at some toys?" asked the storekeeper.

"My little boy thinks he would like the Nodding Donkey in the window," said the lady, whose name was Mrs. Richmond.

"Ah, yes, that is a very fine toy!" said Mr. Mugg, with a smile for the lame boy. "It is one of the very latest from the shop of Santa Claus. Geraldine, please show the boy the Nodding Donkey," Mr. Mugg called, and as Joe, the lame boy, walked along with Miss Geraldine, Mr. Mugg said to Mrs. Richmond:

"I am very sorry to see that your boy has to go on crutches."

"Yes, his father and I feel very sad about it," Joe's mother answered. "We have already had the doctors do almost everything they can to cure him, but now we fear he must have another and worse operation. I dread it, and that is why I would get him almost anything to make him happy. He seemed very pleased with the Nodding Donkey."

"I'm sure Joe will like that toy," said Mr. Mugg.

And when Joe had the wooden animal in his hands, and saw how much faster the head nodded at him, the lame boy smiled and said:

"Oh, this is the nicest toy I ever had!"

"I am glad you like it," said the storekeeper. "Geraldine, please wrap up the Nodding Donkey for Joe."

All this while the Nodding Donkey had said nothing, of course, and he had done nothing, except to shake his head. He took one last look around the toy store as he was being wrapped up in paper by Miss Geraldine. The Nodding Donkey saw the Jack in the Box and the China Cat peering at him.

"I wish I might say good-by to them," thought the four-legged toy, "but I suppose it isn't allowed. I shall be lonesome without them."

The China Cat wished she might wave her paw, or even the tip of her tail, at her friend, the Nodding Donkey, and the Jack in the Box did seem to nod a farewell, but perhaps that was because he was on a spring, and could move so easily. As for the China Cat, she had to keep straight and stiff.

With the Nodding Donkey safely wrapped in paper under his arm, Joe left the store of Mr. Mugg with his mother. Joe limped along on his crutches, and he had to go slowly. But he was smiling happily, and for the first day in a long time he forgot about his lameness. And when his mother saw her son smiling, she, too, smiled. But she was worried about another operation that Joe must go through. The doctor had said that one of his legs had grown so crooked that the only way to fix it was to break it, and let it grow together again, straight.

But now, with his Nodding Donkey, Joe thought nothing about operations, or his crutches, or about being lame. All his mind was on the Nodding Donkey, and he even tore a little hole in the paper so he could look through and make sure his toy was all right.

His mother saw him tearing this hole as they sat in the street car riding home, and as she looked down at him sitting beside her she smiled and asked:

"Aren't you afraid your Nodding Donkey will take cold?"

"Oh, no, Mother," Joe answered. "It is nice and warm in this car. But I'll hold my hand over the hole if you want me to, and that will keep out the wind when we walk along the street."

Soon Joe and his mother left the car, to walk toward their home, which was not far from the corner. The weather was getting colder now, and even inside the wrapping paper the Nodding Donkey could feel it, though the lame boy did hold his hand over the hole.

"I wonder what sort of place I am coming into?" thought the Nodding Donkey, as he felt himself being carried inside a house. Wrapped up as he was, of course he could see nothing. But he could feel that the house was warm, for being out in the cold air was almost like the time he had been tossed from the sleigh of Santa Claus into the snowdrift.

"Now I'll have some fun!" cried Joe, as he took the paper off his toy. "Will you please get me my Noah's Ark, Mother? I'll take the animals and have a circus."

Joe sat down to a table and placed the Nodding Donkey in front of him. Up and down and sidewise bobbed the loose head of the toy. And, as he nodded, the Donkey had a chance to look about him. His new home was quite different from the gay toy store he had been taken from. Here was only a plain house, though it was neat and clean and pretty.

"I think I shall like it here," said the Donkey to himself. "I believe Joe will be good and kind to me. I am going to be lonesome at first, but that cannot be helped."

However, the Nodding Donkey was not lonesome now, for Joe's mother set on the table in front of the boy a rather battered old Noah's Ark. From this Joe took out an elephant, a tiger, a lion, a camel and many other animals. They were not as large or as fine as the Nodding Donkey, and they looked at him in a rather queer way, did these animals from the Noah's Ark. Of course they did not dare say or do anything as long as Joe was looking at them.

"Now I will pretend that this table is the circus ring," said Joe, talking to himself, as he often did. "I will put the Nodding Donkey in the middle and all the other animals around him. Then I'll be the Ringmaster and make believe they are doing tricks."

So Joe put the Nodding Donkey in the very center of the table, where the new toy bobbed his head up and down and sidewise, just as he had done in the store of Mr. Mugg and in the workshop of Santa Claus.

"Now comes the Tiger," said Joe, going on with his circus play, and he set that striped animal down near the Donkey. "And then the Lion. I hope they don't bite my new Donkey."

But the Noah's Ark animals were very good and kind, and they did not so much as open their mouths at the Nodding Donkey. Joe played away and had lots of fun at his pretend circus, while his mother got the supper ready. Once when she came into the room where the lame boy sat at the table, Mrs. Richmond said:

"I just saw some friends of yours going past, Joe."

"Who were they?" asked Joe.

"Arnold and Sidney," was the answer. "Arnold had his Bold Tin Soldier, and Sidney was carrying his Calico Clown."

"Oh, I want to see them!" cried Joe. "They have such fun with their toys, and I want them to come in and see mine."

"I'm afraid it is too late—they have gone on home," answered Mrs. Richmond, but Joe took his crutches, which stood near his chair, and hobbled into the front room, where he could look out in the street to see the boys of whom his mother had spoken.

The Nodding Donkey was left on the table with the other animals from the Noah's Ark. As Mrs. Richmond, as well as Joe, was out of the room, and there was no one to look at them, the animals could do as they pleased.

"How do you do?" politely asked the Lion. "We are glad you have come to live here, Mr. Nodding Donkey. But where is the Noah's Ark that you belong in? It must be very large."

"I did not come out of a Noah's Ark," the Donkey answered, with a friendly nod of his head. "I came first from the workshop of Santa Claus, at the North Pole, and just now I came from a toy store."

"Yes, we, too, were in each of those places, years ago," said the Tiger. "But we have belonged to the little lame boy for a long while. He is very good to us, and you will like it here."

"I heard the boy's mother speak of a Bold Tin Soldier and a Calico Clown," said the Donkey. "Do they belong here?"

"No; they are toys that belong to boys who sometimes come to play with Joe," answered the Elephant. "Then we have jolly times! You ought to see that Calico Clown! He is so funny! And you ought to hear him tell about the time in the toy store when his trousers caught fire!"

"That never happened in the toy store where I was—not in Mr. Mugg's store," said the Donkey.

"No, that was another store," said the Elephant. "You'll like the Calico Clown, I know you will, and the Bold Tin Soldier, too. Arnold and Sidney will bring them over some day."

"Now that I think of it, I believe I have heard those toys spoken of in the workshop of Santa Claus," said the Donkey. "The China Cat also mentioned them. Yes, I should like to see them. But we had better stop talking. I think I hear Joe or his mother coming back."

There was a noise at the door, but it was not made by the lame boy or his mother. They were both at the front window, looking down the street at

Arnold and Sidney, who were going home, one with his Bold Tin Soldier and the other with his Calico Clown.

And then, all of a sudden, something covered with fur and with a big, bushy tail, like a dustbrush, jumped up on the table and sprang at the Nodding Donkey.

CHAPTER VII

THE FLOOD

"Look out there!" roared the Noah's Ark Lion.

"Here! What are you going to do?" snarled the Noah's Ark Tiger.

Of course neither of these animals made very much noise, being quite small, but they did the best they could.

"Come over by me, Mr. Nodding Donkey, if you are afraid!" called the Elephant through his trunk. He was the largest animal in the Noah's Ark, but even he was not as big as the Donkey. As for that nodding toy, he reared back on his hind legs when he saw the strange animal, covered with fur and with the big tail like a dustbrush, jump on the table. The toy animals could move and talk among themselves now, as long as no human being was in the room.

The furry animal stood on the table in the midst of the toys. He sat up on his hind legs and seemed to be eating something that he held in his forepaws.

"Are you a cat?" asked the Noah's Ark Camel, sort of making his two humps shiver.

"No, I'm not a cat," was the answer. "I am a Chattering Squirrel, and I am eating a nut. I live in a hollow tree just outside this house, and, seeing a window open and all you toys on the table, I jumped in to see what fun you were having."

"Oh, that's all right," said the Nodding Donkey politely. "We are glad to see you. But even I was scared, at first. We were just talking among ourselves while the lame boy is away. He was playing circus with us."

"We Are Glad to See You," Said the Nodding Donkey. "We Are Glad to See You," Said the Nodding Donkey.

Page 73

"I know the lame boy," said the Chattering Squirrel. "He is very kind to me. He puts nuts out for me to eat. I am eating one now. Will you have a nibble?" and the squirrel held out the nut to the Nodding Donkey.

"No, thank you; I don't eat nuts," returned the new toy.

"I eat other things, too," went on the Squirrel. "I take them right out of the lame boy's hand, and I never nip him, for I like him and he likes me. I am sorry he is lame."

"So am I," said the Nodding Donkey. "I felt sorry for him when he looked in the store window of Mr. Mugg's shop, and I nodded to him so that he smiled. But hush! Here he comes now!"

And this time it was the lame boy and his mother coming back into the room where the Nodding Donkey and the Noah's Ark toys had been left on the table. Instantly each toy became stark and stiff and no longer moved or spoke. But the Chattering Squirrel, not being a toy, could do as he pleased. So he frisked his tail and nibbled the nut.

"Oh, Mother! See! There is Frisky, my tame Squirrel!" cried Joe. "He must have come in through the window to see my Nodding Donkey. Hello, Frisky!" cried the lame boy, and then when he put down his hand the Chattering Squirrel scrambled across the table and let Joe rub his soft fur.

"I guess he is looking for something to eat," said Mrs. Richmond, with a smile. "He wants his supper, as you want yours, Joe, and as your father will, as soon as he gets home. You had better put away your toys now—your Nodding Donkey and the Noah's Ark animals—and get ready for supper. I think there are a few more nuts left which you may give Frisky."

"Oh, he'll love those, Mother!" cried Joe. And when he had put away his toys he brought out some more nuts for the Squirrel, who liked them very much.

The Nodding Donkey was put up on the mantel shelf in the dining room, but the Noah's Ark toys, being older, were set aside in a closet.

"I want Daddy to see my Donkey as soon as he comes in," said Joe, and he waited for his father. Soon Mr. Richmond's step was heard in the hall, and Joe hobbled on his crutches to meet him. Frisky, the Chattering Squirrel, had skipped out of the open window in the kitchen as soon as he had eaten the nuts Joe gave him.

"How is my boy to-night?" asked Mr. Richmond, as he hugged Joe.

"Oh, I'm fine!" was the answer. "And look what Mother bought me!"

Joe pointed to the Nodding Donkey on the mantel.

"Well, he is a fine fellow!" exclaimed Mr. Richmond. "Where did he come from?"

"From the toy shop," Joe answered, and then, even though supper was almost ready, he had to show his father how the Donkey nodded his head.

"He surely is a jolly chap!" cried Daddy Richmond, when he had taken up the Donkey and looked him all over. "And now how are your legs?" he asked Joe.

"They hurt some; but I don't mind them so much when I have my Donkey," was the answer.

After supper Joe again played with his toy, and, noticing that their son was not listening, Mr. and Mrs. Richmond talked about him in low voices.

"He doesn't really seem to be much better," said the father sadly.

"No," agreed the mother. "I am afraid we shall have to let the doctor break that one leg and set it over again. That may make our boy well."

"I hope so," said Mr. Richmond, and both he and his wife were sad as they thought of the lame one.

But Joe was happier than he had been in some time, for he had his Nodding Donkey to play with. When the time came to go to bed, Joe put the Donkey away in the closet with the Noah's Ark, his toy train of cars, the ball he tossed when his legs did not pain him too much, and his other playthings.

"Well, how do you like it here?" asked the toy Fireman of the toy train, when the house was all quiet and still and the toys were allowed to do as they pleased.

"I think I shall like it very much," was the Donkey's answer.

"I would give you a ride on this toy train," said the Engineer in the cab across from the Fireman, "but you are too large to get in any of the cars."

"But we aren't!" cried the Tiger. "Come on, Mr. Lion, let's go for a ride while we have the chance!"

"All right!" agreed the Lion from the Noah's Ark.

So then, in the closet where they had been put away for the night, the small animals rode up and down the floor in the toy train. The Fireman made believe piles of coal under the boiler, and the Engineer turned on the steam and made the cars go. The Fireman rang the bell, and the Engineer tooted the whistle.

The Nodding Donkey, being rather large, could not fit in the train, but the other toys were just right, and they had a fine time.

"Perhaps if you climbed up on top of the cars I might give you a ride," said the Engineer after he had taken all the Noah's Ark animals on short trips around the closet floor.

"Oh, thank you; but I might fall off and get my head out of order so it would not nod," answered the Donkey. "I think I'll just keep quiet this evening."

"Perhaps you could tell us a story," suggested the Camel. "Tell us the latest news from North Pole Land, where Santa Claus lives. It is a long time since we were there."

"Yes, I could do that," agreed the Nodding Donkey. "And I'll tell you how we ran into a snow bank."

So the Nodding Donkey did this, telling the Noah's Ark animals the same story that I have told you, thus far, in this book. The night passed very happily for the toys in the closet.

When morning came the toys had to become quiet, for it was not allowed for them to be heard talking or to be seen at their make believe fun.

Then began many happy days for the Nodding Donkey. Joe, the lame boy, made a little stable for his new toy, building it out of pieces of wood. He put some straw from the chicken coop in it, so the Donkey would have a soft bed on which to sleep.

Joe played all sorts of games with his new toy. Sometimes it would be a circus game, and again the lame boy would tie little bundles of wood on his Donkey's back, making believe they were gold and diamonds which the animal was carrying down out of pretend mines.

One day Arnold and Sidney, two boys who lived not very far from the home of Joe, came over with their playthings. Arnold brought his Bold Tin Soldier and his company and Sidney his Calico Clown. The three boys looked at the Nodding Donkey and admired him very much, and Joe had fun playing with the Soldier and the Clown.

After a while Mrs. Richmond called to Joe and his chums:

"Come out into the kitchen, boys, and I'll give you some bread and jam," and you can easily believe the boys did not take long to hurry out, Joe stumping along on his crutches.

Meanwhile the Donkey, the Clown, and the Soldier and his men, being left by themselves in the other room, had a chance to talk.

"I am so glad to meet you," brayed the Donkey. "I have heard so much about you."

"Did you hear how once I burned my trousers?" asked the Calico Clown.

"I heard it mentioned," the Donkey said; "but I should like to hear more about it."

"I'll tell you," offered the funny chap. So he related that tale, just as it is told in another of these books.

"Well, that was quite an adventure," said the Donkey, when all had been told. "I suppose you have had adventures, too?" he went on, looking at the Bold Tin Soldier.

"Oh, a few," was the answer.

"Tell them about the time, in the toy shop, when you drew your sword and frightened away the rat that was coming after the Sawdust Doll and the Candy Rabbit," suggested the Clown.

"All right, I will," said the Soldier, and he did. You may read, if you like, about the Candy Rabbit and the Sawdust Doll in the books written especially about those toys.

So the Nodding Donkey listened to the stories told by the Soldier and the Clown, and he was just wishing he might have adventures such as they had

had, when back into the room came Joe and his friends. They had finished eating the bread and jam. Then the boys played again with their toys until it was time for Arnold and Sidney to go home.

And now I must tell you of a wonderful adventure that befell the Nodding Donkey about a week after he had come to live with the lame boy, and how he saved Joe's home from being flooded with water.

Joe had been playing with his Nodding Donkey all day, but toward evening the little lame boy's legs pained him so that he had to be put to bed in a hurry. And in such a hurry that he forgot all about the Nodding Donkey and left him on the floor in the kitchen, under the sink, which Joe had pretended was a cave of gold.

"I wonder if I am to stay here all night! It is growing bitterly cold, too!" thought the Donkey, as Joe's father and mother took their boy up to bed. "They must have forgotten me."

And that is just what had happened. After Joe had gone to sleep his father and mother sat in the dining room talking about him.

"I think we shall have to have the doctor come and see Joe to-morrow," said Mr. Richmond. "His legs seem to be getting worse."

"Yes," answered Mrs. Richmond. "Something must be done."

They were both very sad, and sat there silent for some time.

Meanwhile, out in the kitchen, at the sink, something was happening. Suddenly a water pipe burst. It did not make any noise, but the water began trickling down over the floor in a flood. Right where the Nodding Donkey stood, in the pretend cave, the water poured. It rose around the legs of the Donkey, and he felt himself being lifted up and carried across the kitchen toward the dining room door.

The burst pipe had caused a flood, and the Nodding Donkey was right in it!

CHAPTER VIII

A BROKEN LEG

Had Mr. and Mrs. Richmond not been in the next room, the Nodding Donkey might have kicked up his heels and have jumped out of the stream of water that was running from the burst pipe of the sink across the floor. But knowing people were so close at hand, where they might catch sight of him, the Donkey dared not move.

All he could do was to float along with the stream of water, which was now getting higher and higher and larger and larger. The water felt cold on the legs of the Donkey, for this was now winter, and the water was like ice. So the Nodding Donkey shivered and shook in the cold water of the flood, and wondered what would happen.

Out in the dining room, next the kitchen, sat Joe's father and mother. They were silent and sad, thinking of their lame boy.

They were thinking so much about him, and what the doctors would have to do to him to make him well and strong, that neither of them paid any heed to the running water. If they had not been thinking so much about Joe they might have heard the hissing sound.

But suddenly Mrs. Richmond, who was looking at the floor, gave a start, and half arose from her chair.

"Look!" she cried to her husband. "There is Joe's Nodding Donkey!"

"Why!" exclaimed Mr. Richmond, "it is floating along on a stream of water! The frost has made a pipe burst in the kitchen and the water is spurting out! Quick! We must shut off the running water!"

It did not take Joe's father long to shut off the water from the burst pipe. That was all that could be done then, as no plumber could be had. Mrs. Richmond lifted the Donkey up off the floor and out of the water, drying him on a towel. And you may well believe that the Donkey was very glad to be warm and dry again. He was afraid his varnish coat would be spoiled, but I am glad to say it was not.

"It's a lucky thing we sat here talking, and that I saw the Donkey come floating in," said Mrs. Richmond, when the water had been mopped up. "If I had not, the whole house might have been flooded by morning."

"Yes," agreed her husband. "Joe's Nodding Donkey did us a good turn. He saved a lot of damage. The water in the kitchen will not do much harm, but if it had flooded the rest of the house it would."

Then the Donkey was put away in the closet where he belonged, together with the animals from the Noah's Ark.

"How cold and shivery you are, Mr. Donkey," said the Noah's Ark Lamb, when the Donkey had been placed on the closet shelf, after the flood.

"I guess you'd be cold and shivery, too, if you had been through such an adventure as just happened to me!" answered the Donkey.

"Oh, tell us about it!" begged the Lion. "We have been quite dull here all evening, wondering where you were."

So the Donkey told his story of the burst pipe, and after that the animals went to sleep.

Joe was quite surprised when, the next morning, he was told what had happened. And when the plumber came to fix the broken pipe Joe showed the man the Nodding Donkey who had first given warning of the flood.

"He is a fine toy!" said the plumber.

After this Joe's Nodding Donkey had many adventures in his new home. I wish I had room to tell you all of them, but I can only mention a few.

The weather grew colder and colder, and some days many snowflakes fell. The Donkey, looking out of the window, saw them, and he thought of Santa Claus and North Pole Land.

Joe was not as lively as he had been that day he went to Mr. Mugg's store and bought the toy. There were days when Joe never took the Nodding Donkey off the shelf at all. The wooden toy just had to stay there, while Joe lay on a couch near the window and looked out.

"This is too bad!" thought the Donkey. "Joe ought to run about and play like Arnold and Sidney. They have lots of fun in the snow, and they take out the Calico Clown and the Bold Tin Soldier, too. I wish Joe would take me out. I don't mind the cold of the snow as much as I minded the cold water."

But Joe seemed to have forgotten about his Nodding Donkey. The toy stood on a shelf over the couch where the lame boy lay. Once in a while Joe would ask his mother to hand him down the Donkey, but more often the lame boy would lie with his eyes closed, doing nothing.

Then, one day, a sad accident happened. Mrs. Richmond was upstairs, getting Joe's bed ready for him. Though it was not yet night, he said he felt so tired he thought he would go to bed. On the shelf over his head was the Nodding Donkey.

Suddenly, in through a kitchen window that had been left open came Frisky, the Chattering Squirrel. Over the floor scampered the lively little chap, and he gave a sort of whistle at Joe.

"Oh, hello, Frisky!" said the lame boy, opening his eyes. "I'm glad you came in!"

Of course Frisky could not say so in boy language, but he, too, was glad to see Joe.

"Come here, Frisky!" called Joe, and he held out his hand.

"I guess he has some nuts for me," thought the squirrel, and he was right. In one pocket Joe had some nuts, and now he held these out to his little live pet.

Frisky took a nut in his paw, which was almost like a hand, and then, as squirrels often do, he looked for a high place on which he might perch himself to eat. Frisky saw the shelf over Joe's couch, the same shelf on which stood the Nodding Donkey.

"I'll go up there to eat the nut," said Frisky to himself.

Up he scrambled, but he was such a lively little chap that in swinging his tail from side to side he brushed it against the Nodding Donkey.

With a crash that toy fell to the floor near Joe's couch!

"Oh, Frisky! Look what you did!" cried Joe. But the squirrel was so busy eating the nut that he paid no attention to the Donkey.

Joe picked up his plaything. One of the Donkey's varnished legs was dangling by a few splinters.

"Oh! Oh, dear!" cried Joe. "My Donkey's leg is broken! Now he will have to go on crutches as I do! Mother! Come quick!" cried Joe. "Something terrible has happened to my Nodding Donkey!"

CHAPTER IX

A LONESOME DONKEY

"What is the matter, Joe? What has happened?" asked Mrs. Richmond, hurrying downstairs, leaving her son's bed half made.

Mrs. Richmond, hurrying into the room where she had left Joe lying on the couch, saw him sitting up and holding his Nodding Donkey in his hands.

"Oh, look, Mother!" and Joe's voice sounded as if he might be going to cry. "Look what Frisky did to my Donkey! Knocked him off the shelf, and his left hind leg is broken."

"That is too bad," said Mrs. Richmond, but her face showed that she was glad it was not Joe who was hurt. "Yes, the Donkey's leg is broken," she went on, as she took the toy from her son. "Frisky, you are a bad squirrel to break Joe's Donkey!" and she shook her finger at the chattering little animal, who, perched on the shelf, was eating the nut the boy had given him.

"Oh, Mother! Frisky didn't mean to do it," said Joe. "It wasn't his fault. I guess the Nodding Donkey was too close to the edge of the shelf. But now his leg is broken, and I guess he'll have to go on crutches, the same as I do; won't he, Mother?"

The Nodding Donkey did not hear any of this. The pain in his leg was so great that he had fainted, though Joe and his mother did not know this. But the Donkey really had fainted.

"No, Joe," said Mrs. Richmond, after a while, "your Donkey will not have to go on crutches, and I hope the day will soon come when you can lay them aside."

"What do you mean, Mother?" Joe asked eagerly. "Do you think I will ever get better?"

"We hope so," she answered softly. "In a few days you are going to a nice place, called a hospital, where you will go to sleep in a little white bed. Then the doctors will come and, when you wake up again, your legs may be nice and straight so, after a while, you can walk on them again without leaning on crutches."

"Oh, won't I be glad when that happens!" cried Joe, with shining eyes. "But what about my Nodding Donkey, Mother? Can I take him to the hospital and have him fixed, too, so he will not need crutches?"

"Well, we shall see about that," Mrs. Richmond said. "I'll tie his leg up now with a rag, and when your father comes home he may know how to fix it. I never heard of a donkey on crutches."

"I didn't either!" laughed Joe. He felt a little happier now, because he hoped he might be made well and strong again, and because he hoped his father could fix the broken leg of the Nodding Donkey.

Mrs. Richmond got a piece of cloth, and, straightening out the Donkey's leg as best she could, she tied it up. Then she put the toy far back on the shelf, laying it down on its side so it would not fall off again, or topple over.

Frisky scampered out of the window, back to his home in the hollow tree at the end of the yard. Frisky never knew what damage he had done. He was too eager to eat the nut Joe had given him.

"Now lie quietly here, Joe," his mother said. "I will soon have your bed ready for you, and then you can go to sleep."

"I don't want to go until Daddy comes home, so he can fix my Donkey," said the boy, and his mother allowed him to remain up until Mr. Richmond came from the office.

"Oh, ho! So the Donkey has a broken leg, has he?" asked Mr. Richmond in his usual jolly voice, when he came in where Joe was lying on the couch. "Well, I think I can have him fixed."

"How?" asked the little lame boy.

"I'll take him back to the same toy store where you bought him," answered his father. "Mr. Mugg knows how to mend all sorts of toys."

By this time the Donkey had gotten over the fainting fit, as his leg did not hurt him so much after Mrs. Richmond had tied the rag around it. And now the Donkey heard what was said.

"Take me back to the toy store, will they?" thought the Donkey to himself. "Well, I shall be glad to have my leg mended, and also to see the China Cat and some of my other friends. But I want to come back to Joe. I like him, and I like it here. Besides, I am near the Calico Clown and the Bold Tin Soldier. Yes, I shall want to come back when my leg is mended."

Mr. Richmond, still leaving on the Donkey's leg the rag Mrs. Richmond had wound around it, put the toy back on the shelf. Then he carried Joe up to bed.

"When will the doctors operate on our boy, to make him better?" asked Mrs. Richmond of her husband, when Joe was asleep.

"In about a week," was his answer. "I stopped at the hospital to-day, and made all the plans. Joe is to go there a week from to-day."

"Will his Nodding Donkey be mended by that time?" asked Mrs. Richmond. "I think Joe would like to take it to the hospital with him."

"I'll try to get Mr. Mugg to finish it so Joe may have it," said Mr. Richmond. "Poor boy! He has had a hard time in life, but if this operation is a success he will be much happier."

All night long the Nodding Donkey lay on the shelf, his broken leg wrapped in the cloth. He did not nod now, for, lying down as he was, his head could not shake and wabble. Besides, the toy felt too sad and was in too much pain to nod, even if he had stood on his feet. But of course he couldn't stand up with a broken leg. Indeed not!

In the closet, where they were kept, the animals from Noah's Ark talked among themselves that night.

"Where is the Nodding Donkey?" asked the Lion. "Why is he not here with us?"

"I hope he hasn't become too proud, because he is a new, shiny toy and we are old and battered," said the Tiger sadly.

"Nonsense!" rumbled the Elephant. "The Nodding Donkey is not that kind of toy. He would be here if he could. Some accident has happened, you may depend on it."

"Well, I'm glad my train didn't run over him," said the Engineer of the toy locomotive.

"It was some kind of accident, I'm sure," insisted the Elephant. "I heard Joe cry out, and his mother came running downstairs."

And it was an accident, as you know. All night the Nodding Donkey lay on the shelf in the dining room. He had no other toys to talk to, and perhaps it was just as well, for he did not feel like talking with his broken leg hurting him as it did.

Early the next morning Mr. Richmond was on his way to the office, taking the Nodding Donkey with him.

"Let me see him once more before you take him to the toy shop to be fixed!" begged Joe, who had been told what was to be done with his plaything.

Joe's father put the Nodding Donkey into his son's hands.

"Poor fellow!" murmured Joe, gently touching the broken leg. "You are a cripple like me, now. I hope they make you well again."

Then, with another kind pat, Joe gave the Donkey back to his father, and, a little later, Mr. Richmond walked into Mr. Mugg's store with the toy.

"Hum! Yes, that is a bad break, but I think I can fix it," said the jolly old gentleman.

"Let me see," begged Miss Angelina, peering over her father's shoulder, with a dustbrush under her arm. She had been dusting the toys ready for the day's business.

"The leg isn't broken all the way off," said Miss Geraldine, who was washing the face of a China Doll, that, somehow or other, had fallen in the dust.

"Yes, that is a good thing," observed Mr. Mugg. "I can glue the parts together and the Donkey will be as strong as ever. Leave it here, Mr. Richmond. I'll fix it."

"And may I have it back this week?" asked the other. "My boy is going to the hospital to have his legs made strong, if possible, and I think he would like to take the Donkey with him."

"You may have it day after to-morrow," promised the toy man.

The Nodding Donkey was still in such pain from his broken leg that he did not pay much attention to the other toys in the store. But Mr. Mugg lost no time in getting to work on the broken toy.

"Heat me the pot of glue, Geraldine," he called to his daughter, "and get me some paint and varnish. When I mend the broken leg I'll paint over the splintered place, so it will not show."

The Nodding Donkey was taken to a work bench. Mr. Mugg, wearing a long apron and a cap, just like the workmen in the shop of Santa Claus, sat down to begin.

With tiny pieces of wood, put in the broken leg to make it as strong as the others that were not broken, with hot, sticky glue, and with strands of silk thread, Mr. Mugg worked on the Nodding Donkey. The toy felt like braying out as loudly as he could when he felt the hot glue on his leg, but he was not permitted to do this, since Mr. Mugg was looking at him. So he had to keep silent, and in the end he felt much better.

"There, I think you will do now," said Mr. Mugg, as he tightly bound some bandages on the Donkey's leg. "When it gets dry I will paint it over and it will look as good as new."

The mended Donkey was set aside on a shelf by himself, and not among the toys that were for sale. All day and all night long he remained there. He was feeling too upset and in too much pain to be lonesome. All he wished for was to be better.

In the morning he was almost himself again. Mr. Mugg came, and, finding the glue hard and dry, took off the bandages. Then with his knife he scraped away little hard pieces of glue that had dried on the outside, and the toy man also cut away some splinters of new wood that stuck out.

"Now to paint your leg, and you will be finished," said Mr. Mugg.

The smell of the paint and varnish, as it was put on him, made the Nodding Donkey think of when he had first come to life in the workshop of Santa Claus. He was feeling quite young and happy again.

"There you are!" cried Mr. Mugg, as he once more set the Donkey on the shelf for the paint and varnish to dry. And this time the Donkey was allowed to be among the other toys, though he was not for sale.

That night in the store, when all was quiet and still, the Nodding Donkey shook his head and spoke to the China Cat, who was not far away.

"Well, you see I am back here again," said the Nodding Donkey.

"Have you come to stay?" asked the China Cat. "You can't imagine how surprised I was when I saw you brought in! But what has happened?"

Then the Donkey told of his accident, and how he had been mended.

"Your leg looks all right now," said the China Cat, glancing at it in the light of the one lamp Mr. Mugg left burning when he closed his store.

"Yes, I am feeling quite myself again," said the Donkey. "But I am not here to stay. I must go back to Joe, the lame boy."

"At least we shall have a chance to talk over old times for a little while," said the China Cat. "I came near being sold yesterday. A lady was going to buy me for her baby to cut his teeth on. Just fancy!"

"I don't believe you would have liked that," said the Donkey.

"No, indeed!" mewed the China Cat. Then she and the Donkey and the other toys talked for some hours, and told stories. On account of his paint not being dry the Donkey did not walk around, jump or kick as he had used to do.

In the morning the toys had to stop their fun-making, for Mr. Mugg and his daughters came to open the store for the day. And in the afternoon Mr. Richmond called to get the mended toy.

And you can imagine how glad Joe was to get his Donkey back again.

"I'll never let Frisky break any more of your legs," said Joe, as he hugged the Donkey to him. "I'll take you to bed with me to-night."

But though Joe was allowed to take his Donkey to bed with him, it was thought best not to send the toy to the hospital with the little boy, when he went early the next week.

"Good-by, Nodding Donkey!" called Joe to his toy, as he was driven away; and when Mrs. Richmond put the mended Donkey away on the closet shelf, there were tears in her eyes.

The Nodding Donkey knew that something was wrong, but he did not understand all that was happening. He had seen Joe taken away, and he saw himself put in the closet with the Noah's Ark animals.

"What is the matter?" asked the Lion. "Is Joe tired of playing with you, as he grew tired of us?"

"I hope not," said the Nodding Donkey sadly.

But as that day passed, and the next, the Nodding Donkey grew very lonesome for Joe, for he had learned to love the little lame boy.

CHAPTER X

JOE CAN RUN

About a week after Joe had been taken to the hospital, where he had been put in a little white bed, with a rosy-cheeked nurse to look after him, there came a knock on the door of the house where Joe lived, and where the Nodding Donkey also had his home.

"Is Joe here?" asked a little girl named Mirabell, who carried in her arms a toy Lamb on Wheels.

"Joe? No, dear, he isn't here. He is in the hospital having his lame legs fixed," answered Mrs. Richmond. "Didn't you hear about his going away?"

"No," answered Mirabell, "I didn't. But Sidney said Joe had a Nodding Donkey, and I brought my Lamb on Wheels to see the Donkey."

"That is very kind of you," said Mrs. Richmond. "Come in. We are quite worried about Joe, and we hope he will get well and strong so he can run about. But it will be some time yet before he comes from the hospital."

Mirabell entered the house with her Lamb on Wheels. The little girl looked sad when she heard about Joe, but a smile came over her face when she saw the Nodding Donkey, which Joe's mother brought from the closet.

"Oh, what a lovely Donkey!" cried Mirabell. "See, Lamb!" and she held up her toy. "Meet Mr. Nodding Donkey!"

The Donkey nodded his head, but the Lamb could not do that. However, she looked kindly at the nodding toy.

While Mirabell was playing with her Lamb and the Donkey there came another knock on the door of Joe's house.

"It is Herbert with his Monkey on a Stick," said Mrs. Richmond. "Come in," she added, as she opened the door.

"Is Joe back yet?" asked Herbert, after he had said "hello" to Mirabell and put his Monkey toy on the table.

"No, Joe is still in the hospital," answered the lame boy's mother. "He will be home in about three weeks, we hope. Here is his Nodding Donkey toy."

"Oh, that's fine!" cried Herbert. "Arnold told me about it, and I wanted to see it. My mother told me about Joe going to the hospital, and I came to see how he was."

"It is very kind of you," said Joe's mother. "Now I'll leave you children to play with your toys awhile, until I call up the hospital on the telephone and see how Joe is to-day. I have not had a chance to visit him yet."

Herbert and Mirabell had fun playing together, and with the Lamb on Wheels, the Monkey on a Stick, and the Nodding Donkey. After a while the children were given some bread and jam by Mrs. Richmond, who called them into another room to eat it.

"I heard from the hospital that Joe is much better to-day," said Mrs. Richmond, as she spread more bread and butter for her little visitors.

While they were left in the room by themselves, the toys spoke to one another.

"You are a new one, aren't you?" asked the Lamb of the Donkey.

"Yes," was the answer. "Joe got me only a little while before he was taken to the hospital, wherever that is. I guess I was in the hospital myself, when I had my broken leg mended."

"Oh, tell us about it!" begged the Monkey, as he climbed to the top of his stick and slid down again.

So the Donkey told how Frisky had knocked him off the shelf, breaking his leg.

"And Joe had something the matter with his legs, too, so that's why he had to go to the hospital," added the Donkey, as he finished his story. "I do hope he comes back soon, for I am lonesome without him."

The toys spent a happy half hour together, and then when Mirabell and Herbert came back into the room, having finished their bread and jam, the Donkey, the Lamb, and the Monkey had to become quiet.

"We'll come over again, when Joe gets home," said Mirabell, as she and Herbert left.

"And we'll get the other boys and girls and give him a toy party," added the owner of the Monkey.

"Oh, that will be lovely!" said Mrs. Richmond.

The Nodding Donkey was put back in the closet, where he told the Noah's Ark animals all about the visit of the Monkey and Lamb.

"I have heard of those toys," said the Elephant. "They know the Sawdust Doll, the White Rocking Horse, the Candy Rabbit, and the Bold Tin Soldier."

"My, what a lot of jolly toys there are!" said the Donkey. And then he grew silent, thinking of poor little Joe in the hospital.

Joe did not have an easy time. He was very ill and in great pain, but the kind doctors and nurses looked well after him, and his father and mother went to see him almost every day. One afternoon, when Joe had been in the hospital for what seemed to him a whole year, his father and the doctor came into the room. There was also a nurse, and she began to put on Joe the clothes he wore in the street.

"What is going to happen?" asked the boy.

"I am going to take you home, and give your mother a joyful surprise," said his father.

"Oh, how glad I am!" cried Joe. "And then I can see my Nodding Donkey, can't I? Is he all right, Daddy?"

"As right and as fine as ever," answered Mr. Richmond.

Joe could hardly sit still during the ride home. He got out of the automobile and went through the snow up to the front door. His father opened it, and Joe saw his mother standing at the end of the hall.

For a moment Mrs. Richmond could hardly believe what she saw.

"Joe! Joe, my little boy!" she cried. "Oh, you have come home again! Are you all right? Are your legs better? Can you walk?"

"Can I walk, Mother!" cried Joe, in a happy voice. "Of course I can! I can walk without my crutches, and I can run! I can run! See!"

And with that Joe ran down the hall and into his mother's arms.

Oh, what a joyful happy time there was! Joe's legs were straight and strong again, and he did not need his crutches any more.

"And now where is my Nodding Donkey?" he asked. "I want to see him!"

"I'll get him for you," offered his mother, and when the toy was set on the table near Joe, it nodded its head to welcome him home.

"Oh, my dear Donkey! how I missed you while I was in the hospital," said Joe.

"And I missed you, too," thought the Donkey.

Two or three days after this, when Joe had gotten used to being at home again, there came a knock at the door. Outside happy voices were talking and laughing.

When Joe opened the door there stood Dorothy with her Sawdust Doll, Dick with his White Rocking Horse, Arnold with his Bold Tin Soldier, Mirabell with her Lamb, Madeline, who had a Candy Rabbit, Herbert, who carried a Monkey on a Stick, and Sidney with the Calico Clown.

"Surprise on Joe! Surprise on Joe!" cried the children. "We have come to make a Toy Party for you and your Nodding Donkey!"

"Oh, how glad I am!" Joe laughed. "Look at my legs!" he went on. "They are straight now, and I don't have to go on crutches. And my Nodding Donkey, who had a broken leg, is well, too! He doesn't have to go on crutches, either!"

"Hurray!" cried Dick, and all the other boys and girls said: "Hurray! Hurray! Hurray!"

Then the Toy Party began, and the children and the toys had so much fun that it would take three books just to tell about half of it. Joe and his Nodding Donkey were the guests of honor, and all the others tried to make them feel happy. And Joe was happy! One look at his smiling face told that.

As for the Nodding Donkey, you could tell by the way he moved his head that never, in all his life, had he had such a good time.

When Mrs. Richmond called the children to the dining room to eat, the toys were left by themselves in a playroom.

"Ladies and Gentlemen," said the Calico Clown in his jolly voice, "we have all met together, after a long time of being apart. We have all had good times together, and now I hope you will all agree with me when I say that we are glad to welcome the Nodding Donkey among us."

The Nodding Donkey is Welcomed by the Calico Clown. The Nodding Donkey is Welcomed by the Calico Clown.

"Yes, he is very welcome," said the Sawdust Doll. "We are glad he has come to live in this part of the world."

"I am glad of it myself," said the Nodding Donkey. "I never knew, while I was in the workshop of Santa Claus, that so many things could happen down here. Yes, I am very happy that I came. There is only one thing I wish."

"What is that?" asked the Monkey.

"I wish the China Cat were here," said the Donkey. "She lives in Mr. Mugg's store, and I'm sure you would all like her, she is so clean and white."

"Three cheers for the China Cat!" called the Bold Tin Soldier, waving his sword.

And the toys cheered among themselves.

"Tell me more about this China Cat," begged the Candy Rabbit to the Donkey. "Is she anything like me?"

The Nodding Donkey was just going to tell about the China Cat when Joe and the other children came trooping back into the room, having finished their lunch.

"Now let's play circus!" cried Joe. "We have a lot of toys and animals now. Let's play circus."

And so they did. But as there is a story to tell about the China Cat, and as I have no room in this book, I will make up another, and it will be all about the Nodding Donkey's friend, the white China Cat, and how she had many adventures, but managed to keep herself clean.

As for Joe and his friends, they had a very Merry Christmas and a Happy New Year, and the Nodding Donkey lived for a long while after that, happy and contented, and he never even had so much as a pain in the broken leg that Mr. Mugg had mended so nicely.

THE END